S0-AGJ-474

I SPY
A DINOSAUR'S EYE

For Ziggy,
with extra thanks
to Dan
— J.M.

To Abigail Helt
— W.W.

Text copyright © 2003 by Jean Marzollo.
"Tiny Toys," "Odds & Ends," "Toy Chest," and "At the Beach" from *I Spy* © 1992 by Walter Wick; "The Toy Box Solution" and "The Hidden Clue" from *I Spy Mystery* © 1993 by Walter Wick; "City Blocks" from *I Spy Fantasy* © 1994 by Walter Wick; "Patterns and Paint" from *I Spy School Days* © 1995 by Walter Wick; "A Secret Cupboard" from *I Spy Spooky Night* © 1996 by Walter Wick.

ISBN-13: 978-0-439-52471-1
ISBN-10: 0-439-52471-7

39 38 37 36 35   11

Printed in the U.S.A. 40 • This edition first printing, May 2008

I SPY
A DINOSAUR'S EYE

Riddles by Jean Marzollo
Photographs by Walter Wick

Cartwheel
·B·O·O·K·S·®

SCHOLASTIC INC.

New York   Toronto   London   Auckland   Sydney
Mexico City   New Delhi   Hong Kong   Buenos Aires

I spy

 a ball,

 a bear,

 a B,

and a very small

 Statue of Lib

I spy

a palm tree,

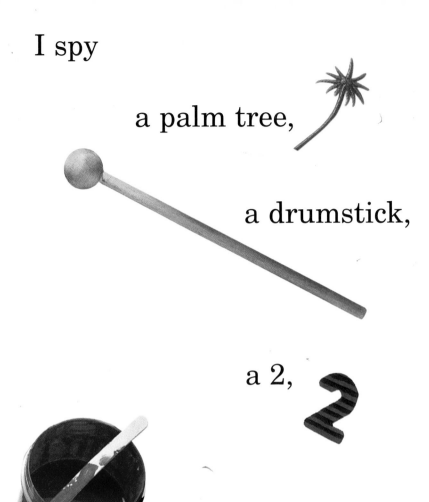

a drumstick,

a 2,

a jar of red paint,

and a cow that can moo.

I spy

an angel,

a dragon,

 a Q,

an egg split in half,

and a hat that is blue.

I spy

a green light,

 two blocks,

a 2,

 an old toy ship,

and a 4 of bones, too.

I spy

a magnet,

 a metal key,

a boat,

 a barrette,

an M, and a V.

I spy

a surfboard,

a rake,

a sail,

the letter A,

and a frog in a pail.

a caboose,

 a dinosaur's eye,

a large yellow e,

and a plane that can fly.

I spy

a bulldozer,

a golf ball,

a hoe,

a rope to jump,

and a man who can throw.

I spy

a rubber band

a bite,

 a J,

a deputy's badge,

 and the letter A.

I spy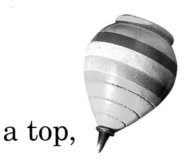

a top,

a small saxophone,

 a large yellow eye,

and a horse all alone.

I spy two matching words.

small saxophone

 ball

very small Statue of Liberty

I spy two matching words.

plane that can fly

bear

man who can throw

I spy two words that start with the letters DR.

drumstick

 palm tree

dragon

I spy two words that start with the letter H.

hat that is blue

angel

horse all alone

I spy three words that end with the letter T.

 green light

 magnet

boat

ball

I spy two words that end
with the letter P.

top

bear

old toy ship

I spy two words that rhyme.

palm tree

 metal key

drumstick

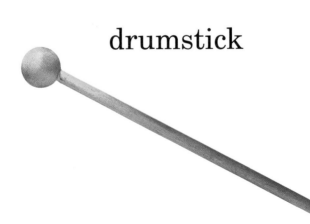

I spy two words that rhyme.

cow that can moo

boat

hat

I SPY™

I SPY, You SPY, Let's all play I SPY!

SEARCH!

New I SPY video games include Ultimate I SPY for Wii™. A revolutionary way to play I SPY!

ESRB Rating: E for Everyone

PLAY!

New puzzles and games from

BRIARPATCH including I SPY Ready Set Silhouette and I SPY Flip 5!

WATCH!

Airs daily on

HBO Family

For more I SPY Fun, log onto
www.scholastic.com/ISPY